GIRLS SURVIVE

Girls Survive is published by Stone Arch Books, an imprint of Capstone.
1710 Roe Crest Drive
North Mankato, Minnesota 56003
www.capstonepub.com

Library of Congress Cataloging-in-Publication Data

Names: Walsh, Jenni L., author. | Pica, Jane, illustrator.
Title: Hettie and the London Blitz : a World War II survival story /
by Jenni L. Walsh ; illustrated by Jane Pica.
Description: North Mankato, Minnesota : Stone Arch Books, 2021. | Series:
Girls survive | Audience: Ages 8-11. | Audience: Grades 4-6. | Summary:
After helping prepare their London home for German bombing raids, young
Hettie and her brothers are sent to safety in the countryside, where she strives
to keep them connected to each other and their parents.
Identifiers: LCCN 2020032588 (print) | LCCN 2020032589 (ebook) |
ISBN 9781515882244 (hardcover) | ISBN 9781515883333 (paperback) |
ISBN 9781515892014 (pdf)
Subjects: CYAC: Family life—England—London—Fiction. | Survival—Fiction. |
World War, 1939-1945—Great Britain—Fiction. | London (England)—
History—Bombardment, 1940-1941—Fiction. | Great Britain—History—
George VI, 1936-1952—Fiction.
Classification: LCC PZ7.1.W3577 Het 2021 (print) | LCC PZ7.1.W3577 (ebook) |
DDC [Fic]—dc23
LC record available at https://lccn.loc.gov/2020032588
LC ebook record available at https://lccn.loc.gov/2020032589.

Image Credits:
Shutterstock: Cosid (geometric background), Spalnic (paper texture background)

Designer: Kayla Rossow

HETTIE
AND THE
LONDON BLITZ

A World War II
Survival Story

by Jenni L. Walsh

illustrated by Jane Pica

STONE ARCH BOOKS
a capstone imprint

CHAPTER ONE

North London, England
Hettie's school
Friday, July 14, 1939

The gas mask I held was lighter than I'd imagined it would be for something that would cover my entire face. In our schoolyard, I stood in line until it was my turn to get fitted.

I didn't *want* to get fitted for a gas mask. All I could think about was how the masks had transformed my classmates into something Martian-like. It was as if they were from another planet, with too-big eyes and a cylinder where their mouths should've been. And I would look just as scary.

It was my turn. I didn't move.

My best friend was beside me in line. Judy hesitated just like me.

"Girls," Mrs. Wallace said. "Step forward, please."

We obeyed, taking smaller steps than usual. I stood in front of Mrs. Wallace while Judy stopped in front of another teacher.

"Okay," Mrs. Wallace began, "I want you both to hold your masks like this." Her own mask was positioned in front of her face with her thumbs inside the straps.

We copied her.

"Good. Now, hold your breath."

We each sucked in a shaky breath of air.

Mrs. Wallace then instructed us to thrust our chins forward into the mask and pull the straps over our heads. One strap wrapped just above my ears, tugging painfully at my hair. Another strap followed the part in my hair.

"Good," Mrs. Wallace said again.

I still held my breath. Looking through the smudged plastic, I dropped my gaze to the grass, not looking at Judy. The others had been transformed. Now I had been too.

While the other teacher helped Judy, Mrs. Wallace pulled on my mask's straps. She pulled tighter, then even tighter, until a satisfied smile appeared on her face. My mask wasn't going anywhere, and, more importantly, nothing could get in or out.

"All set," she said. "Go ahead and take a breath, Hettie."

I did, and, boy, was it startling! The rubbery smell filled my nostrils, making my nose twitch. There was also a weird, uncomfortable sensation. When I breathed in, I fought for air through the filter over my mouth. And as the air came through, my skin was sucked into the mask like a vacuum.

Without meaning to, my hands jumped toward the gas mask to pull it away from my suctioned face, but Mrs. Wallace caught them.

I breathed out, and the suction broke. I didn't want to inhale again, but what choice did I have? My face sucked in. Then out. Then in. And out again.

I hated every second of it. "Can I take this off now?" I asked.

I didn't sound like myself. Beside me, I sensed Judy jump from my strange, robotic voice. I still didn't want to look at her.

"You should wear your mask a bit," said Mrs. Wallace. "That way you can get used to it."

Some of the other kids already were trying to do that, chasing each other around the playground. But I had no desire to get used to wearing a gas mask. I only wanted it off. Not only because this thing was horrible, but also because the reason we were getting fitted for masks was horribly scary.

Everyone—my parents, my teachers, my neighbors, even the man at the grocer—talked about how they feared war between us and Germany. At first, the adults spoke like they were undercover agents. Mum and Dad spelled out words, apparently forgetting that I was twelve and Oliver was nine. Only George, my youngest brother, couldn't spell yet. He was four.

But now, the adults spoke more freely. They said there was a German man named Adolf Hitler who controlled an army that was invading other countries. They also said Great Britain would have no choice but to declare war on Germany if Hitler invaded Poland. Great Britain consisted of the countries of Wales, Scotland, and England, where I lived. The country of Poland was an ally of Great Britain.

At breakfast a few days ago, Mum had said to Dad, "Adolf Hitler has annexed parts of Czechoslovakia, Austria, and France."

"Right," Dad had said. "He made those countries part of Germany because he wants all German-speaking people to be part of their empire."

"And Prime Minister Chamberlain agreed to it to avoid another war," Mum had continued. "Our military still hasn't fully recovered from the Great War against Germany. I understand all of that. But what does Adolf Hitler want with Poland? There are hardly any German-speaking people there."

Dad had shaken his head. "Power. Greed. He agreed not to invade Poland, but I don't trust him." At our table, Dad had held up a flyer that was called *Public Information Leaflet No. 1*. It read: Some things you should know if the war should come.

My dad wasn't the only person who didn't trust Adolf Hitler.

The flyer talked about how a war with Germany could lead to them bombing us. How it could cause fires. How the bombs could be filled with poisonous gas. If this happened, bells would ring. Because of all of this, the leaflet said there'd be a voluntary evacuation of children from parts of England. This way kids wouldn't be involved in these air raids.

Mum had been very quick to say no. My brothers and I wouldn't be evacuated.

Good, I had thought.

Evacuating was the last thing I wanted to do. During these evacuations, children would usually be taken to the countryside. Their parents would remain in London. That would split up our family.

Remembering the conversation almost brought me to my knees, right there in the schoolyard. I shook away the memory, but it felt all too real. The part about poisonous gases was especially real, considering a protective gas mask was now covering my face.

I ripped off the mask, ignoring the pain as it tore at my hair. The inside of the mask was wet from the moisture of my breath. We were told to wipe the mask with a dry cloth before putting it back in its box and keeping it with us.

I only wanted it put away. Forever.

Judy took hers off too, but she obediently untucked her shirt from her skirt to wipe her mask clean. The whole time, she looked like she was going to be sick.

I didn't feel so good either. "Can we go home now?" I asked Mrs. Wallace. We technically had another twenty minutes of school left. But still Mrs. Wallace paused from helping one of my classmates. She squeezed my arm and nodded.

Judy and I left as quickly as possible. We carried our school bags and face mask boxes as we walked down the sidewalk. On the sides of buildings and in shop windows, we passed posters about the upcoming voluntary evacuations. We passed flyers encouraging men to volunteer to be air raid wardens.

I never looked at the posters or flyers long enough to read the details.

Judy said only one thing the entire walk home, her word coming out almost like a shudder. "Scary."

"It is," I said.

Outside our attached houses, known as rowhomes, Judy and I split ways. We offered each other a quick wave.

Usually I skipped from one stone to another on the footpath to our front door, but today I wasn't in the mood. It was one of those days where I wanted to sink into Mum's arms and have her tell me that everything was going to be okay. I wanted her to say that I wouldn't need my new mask and that this man named Adolf Hitler wasn't going to try to hurt us.

I went inside, about to call out, "Mum, I'm home!" But there was no need to announce myself. Mum was in our small living room. So was Dad. My eyes went wide at the sight of him.

Why was Dad home this early? He was supposed to be working at the factory.

And what was he holding in his hands?

CHAPTER TWO

North London, England
Hettie's home
Friday, July 14, 1939

"Dad?" I asked. "What's that?"

He held what almost looked like an oversized blank canvas with a frame for painting. Except what Dad held wasn't white. It was black. It couldn't be used for painting. Besides, Dad didn't paint.

"Hettie," Dad said, talking around two nails sticking out of his mouth, "I'm glad you're home early. We could use your help."

I set down my school bag and face mask. My question came out slowly. "My help with what?"

Mum said, "We received a second flyer today."

"A second flyer?" I parroted. We'd received *Public Information Leaflet No. 1* only a few days ago. And here was another flyer? In the same month? I was almost too afraid to ask, "What's this one say?"

Mum answered, "Part of it is about the gas masks and how to put them on."

"I already know how," I said sharply. I instantly regretted speaking to my mother that way and mumbled an apology.

Dad saved me from Mum's glare by raising the black canvas. He removed the nails from his mouth. "The leaflet also said it's time to cover our windows. We need to cover every one so that no light from inside can be seen from outside at night."

"We won't be able to see out?"

Dad nodded. He said, "The key is no one will be able to see *our* lights once I nail these over the

windows down here. Upstairs we'll close our blinds and hang dark sheets on top for good measure."

"But why?" I asked, even while I thought I knew the answer. The word *bomb* hurtled through my head.

"Well . . . ," Dad began. He glanced at Mum, then continued, "What we're doing is called a *blackout*. Everyone in England has to do it at night. All the streetlights will be turned off too. All of London will be pitch black. It'll make it harder for any enemy planes to find their target if they try to . . . bomb London."

There was the word: *bomb*. But Dad also said another word that caught in my head: *if*. *If* they try to bomb London.

"So, it's only a precaution?" I asked hopefully. "Just in case?"

Dad glanced at Mum a second time. "We need to be prepared, yes."

I couldn't help repeating my question from before. "But why?" I licked my lips. "Why is everyone so insistent that Adolf Hitler will invade Poland, that we'll go to war, that London will be bombed?"

It was the first time I said it out loud, all together like that. And it was terrifying to be the one saying it.

Dad propped the canvas against the wall. He followed with a sigh. "Because it's happened before, during the Great War. Germany bombed London several times then. It can happen again."

"But we're not at war," I insisted.

"We're not," Dad agreed. "Not yet. But before the Great War began, Great Britain warned Germany that we'd declare war if they invaded Belgium." Dad raised his arm and let it fall. "Germany invaded anyway."

And now, Great Britain was in the situation again with Germany, this time over Poland.

I was at a loss for words.

Mum wasn't. She told Dad that was enough history talk.

He nodded. "I need you to help your brothers hang sheets over their windows, okay?"

I hesitated, as if me not participating in the blackout would somehow stop Germany from their plans. "Okay," I said finally.

They both offered me tight, reassuring smiles. I wished I felt reassured. I only felt a pit in my stomach that *everyone* felt so certain that these types of preparations were needed.

After dinner, different preparations were underway, now for bedtime. Tonight was my turn to watch Georgie during his bath. This mostly required me sitting on the closed toilet lid and reading a book while he played with his boats in the tub.

I couldn't even look at his boats, imagining battleships instead of harmless plastic toys. Every firing sound he made caused me to cringe.

I wished I was bringing in the clothes from the line, like Oliver was. We traded off chores, our family working like a well-oiled machine. But tonight it was my job to make sure George washed behind his ears.

Mum and Dad were downstairs doing the dishes. It was when they did most of their talking. They often talked about Mum's day or Dad's work at the factory.

But tonight they weren't talking about anything so normal. Their voices traveled up to the second story of our house where I was. I hadn't wanted to listen, but I also couldn't *not* listen. They were talking about the upcoming evacuations.

"Please rethink it," Dad was saying. "I know they aren't mandatory—we can choose if we send the kids or not—but I've seen war, Margaret. I don't think it's the worst idea for the kids to go."

"Go where?" Mum said, her voice laced with anger. "We won't know. Our children will be sent God knows where for God knows how long."

"But they'll be safe."

"Safe? What does that even mean, Charlie? No child is ever fully *safe*."

There was a pause. I pictured Dad's deep inhale. "Dorothy wasn't our fault, honey. She got sick."

I clutched my book and closed my eyes, feeling tears build behind my lids.

Dorothy, my baby sister, got sick.

She went to the hospital.

She never came home.

Part of me always felt like I could've done more. Mum was so busy that morning. I couldn't even remember with what. But I was the one feeding Dorothy. Why hadn't I told Mum she wouldn't eat anything? Why hadn't I touched Dorothy's forehead to see if she was hot?

I sucked in the humid bathroom air.

George played happily in the water.

Downstairs, I heard Oliver come inside with the wash.

If it wasn't for my brothers and me, I doubted Mum would've recovered from the loss of my little sister. Over a year later, I still heard her crying some nights.

Mum's voice came softer. "I just want us all to stay together, Charlie. I can't be separated from any more of my children. I can't."

"Hettie. I'm done," Georgie announced. He had goose pimples on his arms.

"You got behind your ears?"

He nodded. I reached down to pull the plug in the tub, then grabbed him a towel. I held it up, and he stepped out of the tub.

"Brr! It's cold!" he shouted. I rolled my eyes as I quickly wrapped it around him. But as he took a step, he slipped. I was there to catch him.

"I have you," I said.

And I meant it, in all ways. No matter what happened with Adolf Hitler, I knew I had to be there for my family.

I had to make sure we stayed together. I needed to help show Dad that our family would be safe here. That meant no more hesitating when asked to do things, no matter my fears. That meant putting on a brave face.

I made my vow again and again as I followed Georgie into his bedroom to help him get dressed in his pajamas.

Already, the house felt different with all the windows covered. Was it dark outside? I had no way of knowing, unless I pulled aside the sheets and peeked behind my blinds.

I turned off the lights in my bedroom and did just that, just this one time.

Nighttime had fallen. I didn't see a single light. Anywhere. I shuddered.

I was about to turn away, to run to my bedroom light and turn it back on, when I heard something.

It was the growl of an engine. I also caught the sound of voices. But whose? Who was out there in the darkness?

CHAPTER THREE

"Someone's outside!" I called, racing downstairs. Normally, I wouldn't think twice about hearing noises in front of our house. But the blackness put me on edge. I didn't know who was out there.

Downstairs, Mum had a towel slung over her shoulder. Dad was putting away a stack of plates. Oliver had finished with the clothes and was now playing with a toy.

"Who?" Dad asked.

I swallowed, suddenly feeling embarrassed. I regretted running down here like the house was on fire. I had just said I'd wear a brave face. I needed to be calm. I didn't want Dad to worry about me—or my brothers—remaining in London.

Before I could say more, Dad rushed past me, squeezing my arm as he went to the front door. Oliver and I followed quickly behind.

Who and what we found outside wasn't dangerous. In fact, the *what* was quite the opposite. It was something meant to keep us safe. Government workers were delivering bomb shelter kits.

"I'll help you build it tomorrow, Dad," I quickly offered.

I couldn't stop thinking about the shelter as I lay in my bed that night. When the next morning came and Dad, Oliver, and I were laying the steel pieces out across the back garden, the pit in my stomach grew. The instructions were nine confusing-looking steps. A photograph showed the

end result. It was going to take hours of digging.
Once the shelter was built and in place, only half
of it would be visible, with dirt covering even that.
In the half-circle shaped portion above the ground,
there would be a small door to get in and out.
The rest of the shelter would be below ground.
It reminded me of a tomb—one freshly dug.

Creepy.

I didn't want to build it. I would, though, if it
made Dad feel better about us staying together in
London.

I said to him, "This part of the garden is nice
and flat and looks big enough, right?"

Leaning against a shovel, Dad examined the
ground I pointed out.

"Plus," I said, "the shelter will only be a short
distance from the house." I smiled.

He considered, then agreed.

"Looks like it'll be really safe too."

Dad only gave me an "uh huh" as he studied the instructions.

I glanced at Oliver to judge how he was feeling about everything. He was looking over the waist-high fence into Judy's property. They had their own shelter to build. Judy glanced over, and I could tell she was still feeling scared.

I was too. But I reminded myself I couldn't show it. I hoped we never had to use this shelter. I prayed it'd be enough for Dad to keep us in London despite the threat of a war.

North London, England
Underground tube station
Sunday, September 3, 1939

A month and a half had passed, and the war still hadn't come during the summer.

Our bomb shelter looked slightly less ghoulish. The loose dirt that once reminded me of a freshly dug tomb was now covered in grass. It left the shelter looking more like a lump in the ground.

A lump with a door.

I ignored the door. But I feared those thoughts and small comforts were all baloney. Why? Because only two days ago Germany had invaded Poland.

Ever since, I felt like I'd been holding my breath, waiting for my country to declare war in response. But so far nothing had happened—with the exception of the evacuations beginning.

And today, at breakfast, Dad was talking about going to the tube station.

There was an air raid warden location near the underground railroad station, and Dad wanted to volunteer three nights a week.

"What would you do as a warden?" Mum asked him while we ate.

"Patrol the streets and keep an eye on things," he said. "I'd help make sure London is black at night."

The other reason Dad wanted to go to the tube station was because that was where the voluntary evacuations were happening in our neighborhood.

I'd been dreading them all summer, never breathing a word about them, not even to Judy. Her family had decided to stay together in London too. She was an only child, and her mum couldn't let her go.

But many parents felt differently. They had their children pack bags then had said their goodbyes at evacuation locations. These official evacuations had been happening for the past two days.

Today was the final day.

"We'll just go down and have a look," Dad told Mum. "Then we'll decide."

"Then why have the children pack?" Mum countered.

I didn't understand either. Why have me put together a bag with pajamas, a change of underclothes, my gas mask, and some sandwiches? Why have me pin a label to my jacket with my name, school, and where I'd be evacuating from?

I wasn't evacuating. Mum kept insisting as much.

Dad was also insistent that we'd need to pack these belongings anyway, in case London was ever bombed. "We'll keep our bags by the back door, on the chance we ever need to quickly get to the shelter," he went on.

Mum was okay with packing our bags for that reason. Eventually, she agreed to take a walk down to the station.

I agreed too. I packed my bag. Ever since our summer holiday had begun, I'd been focused on showing Dad that the talk of a *maybe war* didn't faze me. I couldn't seem scared. It could be the final thing to convince him to send my brothers and me away.

Even now, as we walked toward the station,
I didn't flick my eyes away from the posters and
flyers that hung everywhere like I once had. I let
my eyes linger on them.

I fought the urge to squeeze my bag against
my chest, and I read the line that said: Leave Hitler
to me, sonny—you ought to be out of London.

No, thank you. Not if my parents couldn't
go too.

At the station, my family saw hundreds of
sobbing families, especially mothers. One mum
screamed as a volunteer tried to take her daughter
from her.

"This is voluntary," the volunteer reminded her.

"I know," the woman said. Still, she wouldn't
release her daughter to be taken away on the
underground train. "Tell me. Where will this
tube take her?"

Did she not know?

I looked up at Mum, unable to hide my fear. Mum pulled Georgie against her. I had assumed parents knew this information. Did they not tell the parents where their children would be taken?

The volunteer answered the woman, "To a train or a bus."

"Then to where?" the woman cried.

She was told, "To safety. You'll receive your child's location once she is placed with a host family." The volunteer's voice sounded both frustrated and tired, as if she'd told a hundred families this same speech.

But how could the volunteer not expect this reaction? I felt Mum's hand slip into mine.

"No," I heard her say over the voices and crying and sounds of a departing tube. Another tube would arrive soon to fill with more children and take them out of London. "No," Mum said again to Dad. "No, Charlie."

No, I screamed in my head.

Dad licked his lips. His eyes jumped from Mum to me, then to Oliver, to Georgie, to the departing tube, and back to Mum. "Okay," he said. "Let's stay together."

My shoulders relaxed. But they wouldn't stay that way for long.

We were barely above ground again when we saw people gathering at storefronts. Within the shops, radios were turned up. The prime minster was talking.

Mr. Chamberlain was saying how Hitler had invaded Poland two days ago. Like during the Great War, my country gave Germany a second chance: Stop or our countries will be at war.

Apparently, like before, Germany chose to ignore it. Mr. Chamberlain announced that Britain was officially at war with Germany.

No.

Dad's face turned white beneath his well-worn brown hat. He'd seen war before. He'd fought in the Great War. It was exactly why he was so worried about my brothers and me staying in London.

"Hitler's actions," Mr. Chamberlain said over the radio, "show convincingly that there is no chance of expecting that this man will ever give up his practice of using force to gain his will. He can only be stopped by force."

We stood in the crowd of people. For a time, no one moved. I braced myself for Dad to change his mind and demand for my brothers and me to get on the next tube out of London.

But before these words came, a siren erupted. It was the siren meant to tell us that Germany's war planes had been spotted in our skies.

CHAPTER **FOUR**

North London, England
Sunday, September 3, 1939

I covered my ears to muffle the whooping sound of the siren. I was too scared to look at the skies, and I clenched my eyes closed.

Dad pulled my hands down. "The siren is just a drill," he said over the whooping noise before pointing to the skies. I was slow to look, but I did. There wasn't a plane in sight.

Okay. Calmer, I followed Dad as he led us toward the nearest shelter. The wait to get inside was long. But soon, as this was only practice, another siren sounded, and we were allowed to go home.

"Who's hungry for a Sunday roast?" Mum asked cheerfully, despite the fact that we were now officially at war. But I understood her happiness because at least we were all still together.

North London, England
Hettie's school
Monday, September 4, 1939

The next day marked the first day of school after the summer holiday. As we always did, Judy and I walked together.

Immediately, things felt different, less than twenty-four hours after the declaration of war. There was a bomb shelter in the corner of the playground now. There were noticeably fewer students walking toward the building. Then there was the huge *something* spread out across the grass outside. It looked deflated. Some type of silver fabric.

"What's that?" I asked Mrs. Wallace.

"It's called a barrage balloon," she told us.

Judy tilted her head. "What's it for?"

"It will be filled with a gas that'll allow it to rise into the sky. Steel cables will keep it anchored, and there's a crank to control how high it goes. The idea," she said, "is for the balloon to keep aircrafts from flying too low."

Aircrafts. "You mean German ones?" I asked.

Mrs. Wallace nodded.

"To keep them from dropping bombs?" Judy asked at barely more than a whisper.

"The balloons can help as a defense, yes. They were used in the Great War as well."

The uniformed workers began to inflate the balloon. My classmates gathered around to watch.

The bell sounded, announcing the start of not only our new school year but also our school day, but our headmaster let us stay outside.

I was eager to watch. The balloon grew larger and larger. Then it rose higher and higher. "Easy

now," one of the men called out. "Let's take care with this wind."

In the end, the balloon reminded me of a blimp, except there was no engine and nobody could ride inside. Not that anyone would want to, not with its purpose to keep bombers away.

With the balloon in the sky, our headmaster finally led my classmates and me inside. Not only were there fewer students but fewer teachers too. So many had evacuated.

As I sat at my desk, I felt nervous remaining in London when so many had decided it was safer to leave and a huge balloon now hovered above our school. I inhaled a deep breath.

Judy noticed. "Me too," she said and reached across the aisle for my hand. She squeezed just as there was a loud *bang*.

The building rattled. Judy and I fell from our seats and onto the floor, still clutching hands. Mrs. Wallace rushed to the window. Shingles and debris rained down. The huge barrage balloon, still filled with air, swayed back and forth just outside. Mrs. Wallace pushed open the window. I heard voices yelling.

"It's all right," Mrs. Wallace said with a hand over her heart. "They were bringing the balloon down because the winds got too strong, and the balloon knocked against the roof. That's all."

That's all, I repeated to myself. *Not a bomb.*

But I couldn't help thinking, *Not yet.*

The first week of school had continued,
thankfully, with no other heart-racing moments.
In fact, an entire year had passed. And as the days,
then weeks had piled up, I'd begun to think the *not
yet* could maybe be *not ever*. Many who had left
London last September even began to return.

Still, I liked to visit Dad at his air warden post to
see if they were worried about a possible bombing.

Today I came with some sandwiches and a jug
of tea. I was happy to see Dad was doing something
so casual as playing cards with the other men. They
were at ease. It put *me* at ease, even while I knew
the war was happening.

My classmates talked about their brothers,
fathers, and uncles who were fighting against
Germany elsewhere, in the sky and in the seas.

I saw the little changes here in London, like how foods like sugar, bacon, and cheese became rationed. And I even knew that Germany's air force, called the Luftwaffe, had bombed England. But those attacks had been outside of London, focused only on military targets. Airfields. Harbors. Aircraft factories. Radar stations.

At least, they had been the targets until a few days ago. There had been a morning attack on the docks along the River Thames in the outskirts of London. That same night, the Luftwaffe had come back. That time, a neighborhood in London had been bombed.

It had been the first time Germany targeted somewhere non-military. They had dropped bombs on regular people. On homes.

This happened kilometers from North London. London itself stretched seventy kilometers from its center, and the docklands were in the southeast.

I had sat in bed, breathless. Even from the other side of London, the sounds of our air force trying to shoot down the German planes had reached me.

Then, the next day, our air force had reacted, retaliating by bombing Berlin, Germany's capital.

But now, two weeks later, Dad was playing an afternoon game of cards with the other men. He was even laughing, even though I was pretty sure he had a losing hand of cards.

Dad pulled me against his side, thanking me for the sandwiches. I looked over his cards. He was indeed losing.

Suddenly, Dad dropped his cards to the table before my brain fully recognized what I was hearing. A siren was going off.

It had begun quiet. The sound grew. It quieted. It grew louder again. It was the air raid siren. *Not yet* had become *now*.

This time, the siren wasn't a drill.

CHAPTER FIVE

North London, England
Saturday, September 7, 1940

Dad rushed us onto the streets. So many people were already there. I saw mouths opening in panic and children with pink cheeks from crying, but all I heard was the wail of the sirens.

My hand was in Dad's, and I clutched it tighter. He was a step ahead of me, pulling me through gaps in the crowd of people rushing down the street toward the public bomb shelter.

My foot caught on a man's heel as I tried to weave around him. Suddenly I lost my balance, and we both went down. My knee hit hard as I landed on the street. I cried out, another sound overpowered by the sirens.

In an instant, Dad was kneeling in front of me, his lips moving. My ears were ringing from all the chaos. I could barely hear him. Dad spoke into my ear, "Are you okay?"

No, I wanted to say, I was not okay. I was so not okay with everything happening around me, I couldn't stand it. But this wasn't the time.

I forced myself to nod. Then he had me back onto my feet.

"We need to hurry," Dad shouted.

Next to us, someone dragged the man I had tripped to his feet. Then he was gone, running toward safety. It was where we needed to be.

Dad tugged on my arm. His urgency made my heart beat faster than I thought it ever could. As we made our way closer to the shelter, we saw that a large crowd had built up by the main entrance.

People from all sides tried to shove their ways through, but it didn't seem like anyone was actually moving forward anymore.

I glanced up at Dad again, and the look on his face made my stomach drop. I had a feeling I knew what it meant.

We might not make it inside in time.

North London, England
Saturday, September 7, 1940

We struggled to get inside with the crowd for several more minutes. The siren continued blaring. "Please!" Dad shouted. "I have a child with me."

Some people let us move ahead of them, but everyone was in such a panic that most didn't even hear him.

Finally, the siren stopped.

Everyone was quiet and still for several long minutes.

The next siren that went off was a steady wailing noise and went on for two minutes. It was the *all clear* that it was safe to return to our homes. A few air raid wardens came over and began speaking to the crowds, but I couldn't hear what they were saying. The blaring still echoed in my head.

"Charlie!" One of the wardens shouted my father's name, drawing us closer. After seeing that we were all right, he said, "We're all clear for now. The bombers aren't coming here. We saw them farther south."

"But in London?" I questioned, unable to keep the fear from my voice.

Dad nodded to the warden, who nodded to me. I reminded myself again to be brave.

I traveled home on shaky legs. Dad walked me there, not leaving my side until he saw that Mum and the boys were fine. Then he immediately returned to his post.

I wished Dad remained with us. I still felt jittery as I went to bed. Last time the Germans bombed London during the day, they came back at night. They could do it again.

And they did.

North London, England
Hettie's home
Saturday, September 7, 1940

It was ten at night when the siren sounded again. They were coming. I tripped out of bed and bumped into Oliver in the hallway.

Already, it felt like we were taking too long.

"We need to hurry," I said, remembering the fright that had shot through me at the thought of not making it into the shelter in time earlier today. Were the planes above us this time?

Together, we raced down the stairs. Mum stumbled down with Georgie. Dad still wasn't home.

We ran outside. It was pitch black. I was careful
not to fall this time, not to waste more precious
time. The siren made its whooping noise. Louder,
then quieter. I heard the planes in the distance. A
cry bubbled up my throat. We made our way across
the garden and toward our shelter. Nearby voices
alerted me to how our neighbors were doing the
same.

"Judy?" I called.

"I'm here," her voice called from her own
garden. If she said anything else, the siren was too
loud for me to hear it.

Then I disappeared down into our shelter to hide
again from the bombs. It was the first time I'd ever
been inside. I hoped it'd be the last. It felt damp and
cold inside the walls. Mum lit a few candles. The
shelter was small. The ground was dirt. There was
a bucket instead of a toilet. The shelter barely fit
the four of us. I bet it'd only be able to fit Dad and

maybe one other person with how half of the space was taken up with a bed and a bunk above it.

The siren stopped. Now all we could do was wait for the second siren to tell us the Luftwaffe's planes were gone.

"Shall we sing?" Mum suggested.

I agreed for the sake of my brothers. But the sound of bombs and planes in the distance kept interrupting our songs.

Finally, Dad arrived. He'd been gone for hours.

Dad's head wouldn't stop shaking in disbelief. "More than seven hundred bombs were dropped. That's what they're saying."

His whispered words were only meant for Mum. In a space so small, there was no way I couldn't hear. It was horrifying to think what was happening to my city.

"Dad," I began. Candlelight flickered over his face, illuminating his worry lines. "What will happen next? Germany has bombed London twice now. Are they done?"

Dad was slow to answer.

"Please?" I prodded.

"I think it'll get worse before it gets better," Dad said. "I think they'll be back."

North London, England
Hettie's school
Monday, October 7, 1940

Dad was right, I thought as I sat at my desk, knitting a blanket for our troops. It did get worse. A month had passed, and each night Germany's planes had returned.

At first, they'd bombed south of my neighborhood. Then the German planes had come to my neighborhood.

Houses here had been hit, but thankfully none on my street so far. Even still, every night my family had taken to going to bed in our shelter before the siren had even begun. We always knew it would.

"Leave the front and back doors open," Dad had told us.

"Why?" I'd asked.

"If we're bombed, the force of the explosion will go out the doors. It could keep our house and those attached to ours standing."

I swallowed at the memory. I prayed we would never have to test that theory.

People began calling Hitler's attack a *blitz* because it was heavy and repeated—again and again. Every single night for the past month.

When would Germany stop? After the Luftwaffe had bombed every neighborhood, street, and home?

The bombings consumed each of my senses. The taste of dust in the air from buildings that had crumbled. The smell of burnt timber. The stuffiness of my home from our windows being unopened for so long. The orange and red skies after a raid. The crunch of broken glass beneath my shoes. The fires eating away the leaves on trees, the bareness making it look like winter had arrived early.

It was all too much.

Our new prime minister gave speeches about how Hitler's intention was to break the confidence of the British people. But Mr. Churchill encouraged us to carry on with our lives during the daytime hours. We went to work. We went to school. In the boarded-up windows of shops, the owners used chalk to write business as usual.

At my desk, I took a deep breath and focused on adding to my blanket. Judy was a better worker— hers already twice as big as mine. Or maybe it was that her mind was focused where it should be, while mine was already busy thinking about tonight's bombing and how close the explosions might come to us this time.

The bombs outside sure sounded close. Too close.

I was stretched out on the top bunk, trying to read a book. It was going as well as my blanket had gone earlier in the day. At least Dad was in the shelter with us tonight instead of volunteering. It was always better when we were all together.

There was a loud *boom*. The ground shook. We all jumped.

Mum's hand covered her heart. Georgie sunk into her. Dad was immediately on his feet. Without a word, he poked his head from our shelter's small door.

"What is it?" I asked him. What I really meant was *what kind of bomb was that*?

A high explosive? A fire bomb? Both?

The Germans would drop high explosive bombs first, to open up a building. Then, fire bombs were dropped to set the building ablaze.

"Both, I think," Dad said.

"In our neighborhood?" Mum asked, but we'd all felt the blast.

"Yes." Then Dad was gone, racing out into the night. He was trained in first aid and putting out fires.

I knew I should close the door behind him, but I couldn't help but watch. The night was glowing. Less than a block away, the attic of a house was in flames.

"We need sand! A ladder!" It was Dad's voice, competing with the roar of the planes' engines above us.

With a hand over my mouth, I continued to watch. Dad raced back toward us. "Inside," he called to me. "There's no time. Get inside!"

As Dad reached our shelter's door, the blast of an explosion pushed him inside. He landed on his knees, knocking into Oliver. Debris clattered overtop our shelter. We stared at each other, wide-eyed.

It was the closest any bomb had ever come to us.

"Have we been hit?" Mum cried.

"I'll check," Dad said.

We all waited nervously, too scared to say anything. Then we heard him groan out, "Oh no."

The rest of us climbed outside to see what had happened. I gasped, dropping to my knees. A bomb hadn't hit our home. It was worse.

A bomb had landed on the shelter next door. *Judy!*

CHAPTER SIX

North London, England
Hettie's family's bomb shelter
Monday, October 7, 1940

I rushed into the red-tinged darkness of the night. Planes roared above me.

Dad was already climbing over the waist-high fence that separated our properties. I did the same.

"Judy!" I called again. A response didn't come.

I knew she'd been inside her shelter with her parents. We'd waved over the fence as we went inside a few hours ago.

My eyes were fully adjusted to the darkness. I saw the lump that once was her shelter. The middle had caved in. There was no longer a door.

I ran toward the lump and began to dig into the dirt and rubble with my bare hands where the door should've been. Oliver was soon beside me.

"It wasn't a direct hit," Dad said. "Thank God. But I need to hurry. Step aside, Hettie." He had a shovel. He sunk it into the ground, using his boot to push it deeper. He heaved the dirt away.

I retrieved a second shovel from Judy's shed. Together, we heaved.

We heaved for what felt like hours. The entire time, I heard no screams or shouts or even cries.

But then, as Dad cleared enough where the entrance to the shelter was visible, I heard moans. "Stay here," he told Oliver and me.

It was so hard to obey. But I did. Dad disappeared into the collapsed shelter. He returned with Judy behind him first.

"Judy!" I rushed toward her. By the time I reached my friend, I had already wiggled free of

my coat. "Here." I put my jacket around her. "Lean on me."

"My parents?" she uttered. My eye caught on a deep cut on her forehead.

Dad answered by pulling free Judy's mum. Judy's dad was last. "Oh, sweetheart!" her mum cried out at the sight of her. Both her parents pulled her into a tight hug.

Somehow, they were all alive. "Everyone all right?" Dad asked, wiping away sweat from his forehead. Judy and her parents nodded. They were okay, save for probably having some bumps and bruises tomorrow. Some bad memories too.

"Back inside," Dad said. He meant inside our family's shelter. "The Luftwaffe are still out there."

"No," Judy cried. "I can't go inside another of those things."

A bomb whistled. I refused to look up. Even if it was dark, the fear of seeing the underbelly of a plane opening and bombs falling out would be too terrifying for me to keep moving.

There was no time to fight Judy on this. I grabbed her hand and pulled her over the fence. "Hurry!" Mum called. She and Georgie were at our shelter's door.

"Wait!" Oliver yelled. His arm was outstretched, pointing.

Dad joined us. "What is it?"

But we all saw it then. Not far from our shelter was a bomb—that hadn't gone off. This happened, I'd heard. Around ten percent of bombs didn't go off. Like this one.

It was as big as I was tall. Some were bigger. Some were twice the height of Dad.

We must've overlooked it when we'd run to save Judy and her family. There was no missing it now.

"Step away," Dad said in a low voice. He looked to Judy's parents. "The underground?"

They nodded. Judy's parents ushered Judy, my brother, and me away from the bomb. Dad quickly went to help Mum and George from our shelter.

I shuddered to think what would've happened if it had gone off and both our families had been trapped underground.

North London, England
Underground tube station
Tuesday, October 8, 1940

Our families descended the stairs to the tube station. At night, it was an underground public shelter. During the day, it would return to its usual purpose: public transportation.

"There must be at least a thousand people down here," I said to Judy.

She chewed on her lip. "How will we all fit?"

We had to make it work. Everyone was crammed in. Much like our shelter, it was damp and cold. But it also smelled like sweat and urine.

Beneath too many bodies, I saw rows of metal beds. I didn't see any bedding, though.

"Where are we supposed to sleep?" I asked Mum.

She didn't answer. Mum only steered us to an unoccupied stretch of wall.

"Go on," she said to us. "Sit down."

At first, my brothers and I didn't move. Normally, Mum would never let us sit on the germ-infested ground in the tube station. But we were all so exhausted.

I sank to the ground, a brother on either side of me. Judy sat next to Georgie. Overtop his head, I saw a trickle of blood oozing from a bandage on Judy's forehead that her mum had quickly put on her.

I felt so relieved cuts and bruises were all my friend had suffered when the bomb had collapsed her shelter.

I stared at a poster. On it, a mother with her children was pictured. Hitler was whispering to her, *Take them back! Take them back!* Larger print said *Don't do it, Mother—leave the children where they are.*

Leave them in the country, where it was safer. I so badly wanted London to be safe for us, but was it?

My backside fell asleep before I did, but I eventually dozed off.

When I woke, Dad was gone. Mum said he left to report the bomb that hadn't gone off in our garden. I shivered, both at the dampness and also at Dad not being with us.

Mum refused to go aboveground until he returned. Other families left. Some stayed, having nowhere else to go, like us.

People needing to take the underground tube to go to work began to arrive. They had to step over those of us on the ground. After muttering sorry seemingly a hundred times, I gave up.

A few other kids had formed a circle, talking and playing a game called jacks. Judy, Oliver, and I joined them.

"Did you hear," one of the boys said, "they had to put to sleep all the poisonous animals at the zoo? People are afraid a bomb will hit their cages and then the animals will escape all over London. Could you imagine?"

The boy ended his story by dropping a small rubber ball, clapping together his hands, and snatching one of the jacks from the concrete ground before the ball landed.

I cringed. I didn't want to hear stories like that. The boy played on as another girl picked up the storytelling.

She said the cemetery across the street from her house had been bombed. "There were rotting bodies and skeletons *everywhere*. They all had to be picked up and reburied."

"Did you help?" Oliver asked.

"Goodness, no! I could barely look at all of it."

The zoo story gave me the chills. This dead-body one was horrifying. Still, there were more stories, including one that really shook me.

"A few days ago," a second boy said, "A boy from my class had his house bombed. His mum, dad, and sister died. Our class clubbed together to buy him a new model car kit. To try to cheer him up. He thanked us, but then the next day he left school. We think he moved out of London to an aunt's house."

I swallowed, knowing that could happen to us. Last night had been eye opening.

Judy and I exchanged worried looks, and my eyes caught again on the bandage along her hairline. Oliver looked nervous too, his bottom lip between his teeth. He was ten. He shouldn't be hearing this, seeing this, *living* this.

None of us should.

I stood to leave the circle, tugging on my brother's shirt to come with me. Mum was standing behind us with Georgie on her hip. She had tears in her eyes. She had overheard everything. "It's time," she said to me.

Behind her, I saw the poster I'd been staring at last night. I knew what she meant. *It's time for you and your brothers to leave London.*

CHAPTER **SEVEN**

As much as it had pained me, I'd agreed to leave. I'd known bombs were tearing apart families in London. I'd also known my family had a better chance of staying whole if my brothers and I left.

Leaving London had been my new way of acting brave. But now my brothers and I were in a place called Clevedon. It was a long way from home. I didn't feel very brave.

Our journey had begun in the tube. Then a steam train. Then a bus. Now we had arrived at a depot. It'd taken half the day.

Dad had arranged everything. The earlier evacuations had been official and put together by the government. Our arrangements were made privately, between Dad and I didn't know who. I supposed people in Somerset because here we were in the countryside.

I'd never been in the country before, with its rolling hills. I saw no barrage balloons in the sky. No planes carrying bombs, either. At least that was comforting.

We stepped off the bus. An older woman waved and beckoned us in her direction. "Hettie, Oliver, George?" she said. Then, "Doris, David, Mabel?"

I looked behind me, not realizing other evacuees had been on our same train. We all nodded.

"Splendid," the woman said. She had a kind face. In the air, I smelled salt from the nearby

Bristol Channel. How different the ocean and countryside smelled from the city. Especially after the city had been bombed. By this point that had happened fifty-six days in a row. Surely, the air raids would stop soon. I told myself we'd only be in Somerset for a matter of days, maybe weeks.

We followed the woman to a church. Once we were inside a large hall, I squeezed my brothers' hands. I was so very knackered. But I felt too nervous to yawn. We were about to meet our host family, the Worthingtons. Unlike the official evacuations, I felt better knowing Mum and Dad knew where we were going and who we'd be with.

While traveling here, I had wondered what the Worthingtons would be like. If Mrs. Worthington would read us bedtime stories like Mum. If Mr. Worthington would tell us jokes over breakfast. If they danced around the living room after they thought the rest of the house was asleep.

I squeezed my brothers' hands more tightly. The other three children, each of them around Georgie's age, were quickly introduced to their host families.

When it was our turn, the adults began to talk quietly among themselves. There were three of them left: the woman who brought us here from the bus, an older man, and an older woman. I assumed the older man and woman were the Worthingtons. They glanced at us. They talked some more. My heart hammered in my chest. What was wrong?

Finally, the woman who'd brought us to the church said, "Children, I'm afraid there's been a mix-up."

I didn't know how to respond to that. What kind of mix-up?

"You see," she went on, "the Worthingtons very graciously offered to take all three of you. Only"—the woman paused—"they didn't realize George was so young."

"He's nearly six," I said. "He's not a baby."

"No," she said. "Certainly not a baby. But the Worthingtons only agreed to take older children."

I heard her words, but I wasn't understanding what this meant. And it made me mad the Worthingtons were simply standing there while someone else spoke for them. I pulled Georgie against me.

Oliver spoke up. "So these people won't take George? They'll take us but not him?"

The great hall was silent. Georgie's head turned up to look at me. Tears filled his eyes.

I shook my head. Then I found my words. "No, you can't split us up. The arrangements my dad made were for all three of us. Georgie stays with us."

The church woman stepped closer. "Of course. We'll find a way to keep George in Clevedon. He'll remain with you and Oliver. George simply won't be *staying* in the Worthingtons' residence."

My head still shook. This wasn't okay. It broke my heart to be separated from my littlest brother. It broke the promise I had made to keep us *together* together. But what other choice did I have?

Clevedon, Somerset, England
The Worthingtons' home
Friday, November 1, 1940

I hated the Worthingtons. I hated that I walked into their stone farmhouse with only one brother.

I hated that Mrs. Worthington had wrinkles above her upper lip, like creases formed because she pursed her lips so often. I hated that the windows were covered even here, where we were supposed to be safer. I hated that Oliver and I were given a quick meal and then immediately asked to help with chores. I hated that Mr. Worthington only watched—and corrected everything I did wrong.

But more than anything, I hated that when I asked Mrs. Worthington if we could check on Georgie before bed, she answered no.

"It's late," she said. "It can wait until tomorrow."

No, it couldn't. *It* wasn't a thing. *It* was my brother. My job was to keep us together. And right now, he wasn't with us. I was told he was with the Howes, whoever they were.

And that was why I had no other choice than to sneak out as soon as Mr. and Mrs. Worthington went to bed.

CHAPTER EIGHT

Clevedon, Somerset, England
Friday, November 1, 1940

The night wasn't fully dark. It would be soon.
I raced against the setting sun, not entirely
sure *where* I was racing. I began on a dirt road,
following a long fence. I felt like a fish out of
water. There was so much space here. More grass,
less concrete.

I stopped short, lost in my thoughts. I barely
heard and, without the vehicle's headlights on
because of the blackout, barely saw the dark
truck that was driving by. The driver honked as
I nervously held a hand over my heart. Then I

thought to call as I approached his window, "Do you know where the Howes live?"

It was a long shot. If I'd asked that in London, the person would look at me like I'd gone mad. There were probably hundreds or maybe even thousands of Howes. But here?

"Ah, Tom and Mary?" the man said. "They live over yonder."

"Where?"

He smiled. "Climb in. It's not safe being out here after dark. I myself almost flattened you with my tires."

The truck's passenger seat felt like it'd been sat in by many people for many years. "Are you the girl staying with the Worthingtons?"

I nodded.

The man raised a brow. "And you're out running about?"

"They don't know."

He whistled at that.

I said, "My youngest brother is at the Howes'.
Mr. and Mrs. Worthington wouldn't keep him."
There was no hiding the bitterness in my voice.

"I see," the man said. "Well, Tom and Mary will
take good care of your brother. That I know."

It was something.

In no time, the man was pointing at a small
cottage. "You hurry back," he told me before I
climbed out. "The Worthingtons won't be happy
you snuck off."

I shrugged at that, thanked him, and turned my
attention to the cottage. The drapes were open. Mr.
Howe was walking toward the window, no doubt to
conceal the light inside now that night had fallen.
Before he got there, I caught a glimpse of Georgie
sitting at the table.

He was crying. It gutted me. It gutted me even
more how Mrs. Howe was rubbing his back.

She stopped to get him a biscuit from a jar, and
he smiled at that. It should've been *me* comforting
my brother.

I knocked forcefully on their door. But as soon
as Mr. Howe opened it, I plastered a fake smile on
my face. It was for Georgie, not them.

My brother barreled into my stomach before I
could say a single word. I wrapped my arms around
him and kissed the top of his head.

"Come in," Mr. Howe said with a small smile. "I take it you're Hettie."

I blushed. It was obvious they knew I'd snuck out of the Worthingtons' house. "Yes," I said quietly.

"And you'd probably like a biscuit too," Mrs. Howe chimed in, opening the jar of baked treats again. "Maybe some tea?"

I wanted to dislike them. But they weren't making it easy for me, especially since—without them—there was no telling where Georgie would be right now.

"Thank you," I said in a weak voice. "And thank you for taking in George."

Mr. and Mrs. Howe exchanged a smile. They were a lot younger than Mr. and Mrs. Worthington. "It'll be a pleasure to have George here. We'll read and play games. He'll have plenty of space to run around."

Part of me wanted to ask if they could take Oliver and me too. But then Mr. Howe said he'd better get me home to the Worthingtons before they noticed I'd gone missing.

I was hesitant to leave Georgie but also knew Oliver was back at the Worthingtons'. I was split between two brothers. Before I left, Georgie sunk his face into my belly again and said, "You'll come see me tomorrow?"

I told him, "Nothing can keep me away."

Clevedon, Somerset, England
The Worthingtons' home
Tuesday, May 13, 1941

I had meant it. Nothing could've kept me away from Georgie, but Mrs. Worthington sure tried. She had caught me sneaking back into her house. My punishment was extra chores. Chores that kept me on the farm longer than I'd liked, and that meant not visiting George until the day was almost over.

But I got to the Howes' every day, all one hundred and ninety-three days that we'd now been in Clevedon.

I now had one hundred and ninety-three letters from Mum. The letters didn't always arrive daily. Some days my heart sank when the post arrived and there was nothing from my parents. But that also meant there were days with two letters. It was like a second helping of dessert.

Dad was busy with his volunteer work as an air raid warden. Mum was a volunteer too, as a nurse. Our house was still standing. Mum and Dad were safe, something I worried about constantly. Judy was evacuated as well, but Mum wasn't sure to where. Once she found out, she was going to let me know.

I wrote them back, telling them about our lives here too.

Oliver used to come to the Howes' with me every day, but he'd made a friend at school and was often off with him playing baseball. It wasn't that Oliver didn't want to see Georgie, he'd told me. But he'd also said, "We don't know how long we'll be here, Hettie. Let's make the most of it. You could make some friends too, you know."

But I didn't.

And with each new letter, I made sure Oliver read it before he ran off with his new friends. Then I'd read it to Georgie. Mum's words felt like a way to keep us together as a family, especially when we'd already spent holidays, birthdays, and so many months apart.

I was changing the bedding in the chicken coop when I saw the postman coming up the drive with today's mail.

"Nothing for you today, Miss Hettie," he said as I greeted him. "But I bet you're happy to hear London wasn't bombed last night."

"It wasn't?" I asked.

The postman shook his head, as if in disbelief. "Haven't been able to say that in months. Last bombing came on Sunday."

And it was Tuesday.

I spat out the question, "Does this mean they're done?"

"Could be," he said with a smile.

I couldn't wait to tell my brothers what I'd learned. When I found Oliver in the fields, I danced him around in a circle. I wasn't done with my chores yet, but I couldn't wait to tell Georgie.

I rushed to the Howes', not bothering to knock. In fact, I hadn't been knocking for weeks now. Mrs. Worthington's home may have been full of photographs of her two sons, but her house felt cold. The Howes' home felt warm and welcoming.

"Georgie!" I called.

"Oh, hi, Hettie," Mrs. Howe said, already veering from whatever she'd been doing to fetch some biscuits for me. "Georgie-pie is out with Tom. You're early today. Have you come with a new letter from your parents? If you can't stay long, I can read it to Georgie later. We've been working on his reading."

"You have?" I asked, and I couldn't help the ache in my stomach. Mum would've jumped at the chance to do this with Georgie, just like she'd done with Oliver and me.

"Why, of course we've been helping him," Mrs. Howe said. "He's certainly school aged. He's six now."

"I know how old he is," I said, a tinge of bitterness in my voice. "But he won't be starting school here."

"Oh, sweetie—" she began.

But I cut her off, saying, "London wasn't bombed last night."

"That's wonderful news!"

"So, I'm sure they'll be sending us home now."

Mrs. Howe didn't answer straight away. She pulled her lip between her teeth. "I never told you how Mr. Howe and I haven't been able to have children, have I?"

I shook my head, not expecting her to tell me this.

"It's been a pleasure to have Georgie here with us. Truly."

Mrs. Howe concentrated on getting something out of the fridge then. I finished my biscuit and said goodbye.

I didn't like leaving without seeing my brother, even if there were traces of him everywhere. An extra set of shoes Mrs. Howe had gotten him. A battleship by the stairs. A train set left on the couch.

As I shut the door behind me, I realized this was the first day that I hadn't seen my brother since we'd been here. I looked back at the Howes' house. Their welcoming and cheerful home. I felt bad thinking it, but it may have been becoming too comfortable for my brother. But that was all about to change. We'd be going home now. We'd be a family again. Soon.

CHAPTER **NINE**

If only that had been true. If only my family would've been reunited *soon*.

The Worthingtons and Howes had both received instructions *not* to send us home, even though the bombings had stopped in London.

"Did my mum and dad say we had to stay here?" I had asked Mrs. Worthington.

"No," she had said. "This is bigger than the both of them."

At least that had been easier to swallow, knowing it wasn't Mum and Dad who had wanted to keep us away. It had been the war keeping us here. Two years later, and the war was still going on.

As we remained in Clevedon, weeks turned to months and to years. It felt like it was getting harder and harder—because of Georgie and because of my promise to keep us together as a family.

He was forgetting Mum and Dad.

I first noticed it when I walked into the Howes' one day and found Georgie laughing with them. *That* wasn't strange. They laughed a lot. I asked him, "What's so funny?"

"We went for a picnic," Georgie began.

Mrs. Howe chimed in. "We had the blanket all spread out."

"Uh huh," my brother went on. "And then, out of nowhere, this red fox came closer."

Mr. Howe laughed, as if expecting what was coming. Georgie and Mrs. Howe laughed too.

Then my brother said, "We didn't think it'd come to the blanket. That's what you said, Tommy."

Tommy? Not *Mr. Howe*?

"But it did!" Georgie exclaimed then. "The fox took my sandwich."

"Then scurried off," Mrs. Howe added. "I bet she had wee ones nearby she was trying to feed."

"They must like ham and cheese," Mr. Howe said with a wink.

They laughed again. I laughed too, but I was playacting. Really, I felt a mixture of happiness and sadness. Happy that Georgie was doing so well away from home, but also sad because, well, he was doing so well.

"Georgie," I said, "remember the time at the zoo when we saw the baby foxes? We all went. Mum, Dad, Oliver, me, you."

Georgie scrunched his face before he shook his head.

"You must remember," I insisted. Years were passing with us in the countryside, but he *had* to have remembered. "You even asked Dad if you could bring one home." I laughed at the memory. Not a full-blown laugh like the Howes and Georgie had done moments ago, but a chuckle—a reaction to a good memory.

Only Georgie didn't remember this memory. How long would it be until he forgot all of our family's stories and replaced them with ones he was making with the Howes? How long would this war go on? How long until we were able to go home again?

Clevedon, Somerset, England
The Worthingtons' home
Monday, May 7, 1945

Oliver wasn't worried that Georgie was making new memories or that Georgie was now in school and Mum was missing it. Oliver had his own new life here too.

It was me whose head was in London but whose body was stuck in Clevedon. I'd never felt so alone, with only my memories to keep me company.

At Mrs. Worthington's kitchen table, I sat, moping.

She let out a long, slow breath. "Hettie, you've been with us years now."

I closed my eyes at that length of time.

"However," Mrs. Worthington said, "I rarely see you happy. What would make you happy?"

The question surprised me, especially the fact that it came from Mrs. Worthington, who rarely smiled herself.

"Being home," I said flatly. Laughing with Judy. Sleeping in my bed again. Having dinner as a family. That would make me happy again.

Mrs. Worthington twisted her lips.

I felt a pang of guilt that I'd hurt her feelings. She wasn't the warmest person, but she had also opened her home to us. She cooked for us. She cared for us. The problem with Mrs. Worthington was that she wasn't my mum.

"If home is what makes you happy, Hettie, then perhaps you should write about it."

"Write about it?" I questioned. "I write to my mum every day." Judy and I exchanged letters now too.

"You do," Mrs. Worthington said. "But what I meant is to write stories about what you remember from home. Here,"—she retrieved some paper from a drawer—"write down what made you happy from home. From before." She glanced at a photograph of two boys.

I'd never asked her about them before, but perhaps Mrs. Worthington saw the question in my eyes. "They're fighting in this war," she revealed. "Both of my sons are fighting for Britain. It's quite hard on me. It's why we offered to take you and

Oliver. We wanted to help in some way. But I knew I wouldn't have the energy for George, for someone so young. I never apologized for that. I'm sorry."

"It's okay," I said. "He's happy with the Howes."

"And I want you to be happy too, Hettie." Mrs. Worthington tapped the paper. "Words can be powerful."

She said it with such confidence that it gave me an idea. It was my job to keep my family together. I felt like I was failing at it miserably. But what if I wrote about home—just like Mrs. Worthington suggested—and read those words to Georgie so he wouldn't forget where we came from?

I smiled and got to work.

I wrote down our memories. I read them to Georgie. I read him Mum's letters too. She still wrote them daily.

One day she wrote how an enclosure at the zoo had been hit by a bomb. A zebra, a donkey, and the donkey's foal escaped, but they were safely rounded up and returned. Mum's story reminded me of another story from the zoo. Georgie had loved the baby foxes, but he had also loved the zebras. So much so that after we'd gotten home, he'd used the coal from the fireplace to draw stripes on himself.

"I did not!" Georgie exclaimed when I read him the story I wrote about that day. He, Oliver, and I were sitting in the Howes' living room with my stack of stories.

"You did!" Oliver said. "I was supposed to be keeping an eye on you. Oops."

The three of us laughed together. I heard Mrs. Howe chuckling to herself from the kitchen. Mr. Howe was in there too, with the radio on.

"Let me see that," Georgie said. His eyes skimmed the page. "Mum scolded me that night in the bath. But I knew she wasn't *too* mad because she was smiling too."

I hadn't written that part of the story down.

"You remember that?" I asked him.

"I remember it all now," he said.

I looked at Georgie then Oliver. "You both remember that day?"

My brothers nodded, and for the first time, I wanted to cry not from sadness but from happiness.

Just then, Mr. Howe came rushing into the living room. His eyes were huge. His mouth opened and closed like a fish.

"What?" I asked him. "What's happened?"

CHAPTER TEN

Clevedon, Somerset, England
The Howes' home
Monday, May 7, 1945

Mr. Howe told us his news, the words tumbling out of his mouth. "They surrendered. Hitler took his own life two days ago. And Germany surrendered. It's over. The Allies have control. The war's over."

My mouth dropped open. The Allies—Great Britain, France, the Soviet Union, and the United States—were now in control of Germany. The war was *finally* over.

It was the only thing keeping my brothers and me from going home. We were going home.

It took another month before it was officially approved for evacuees to return to London. Now Oliver, Georgie, and I were on a train toward home.

Home.

From what Mum told me, our house still stood, remarkably spared by Hitler's bombs. Some of our neighbors hadn't been as fortunate. Beyond our neighborhood, a greater number hadn't been as lucky, especially farther south in central London. In some spots, entire blocks were nothing more than rubble.

Dad wrote how rebuilding had already begun but that we should be prepared for the city to look and feel different.

The day we had stepped off the bus in Clevedon, Georgie had been five, Oliver ten, and I had been thirteen. I was eighteen years old now. It was almost too baffling to comprehend how much time had passed, and I had lived each and every day of it. Days where so much had changed.

Georgie could read and write. Mum had missed him losing most of his front baby teeth and growing in the adult ones. Now there were just a couple loose teeth in the back to go.

Oliver had grown over thirty centimeters taller. His voice had become deeper. He was now smelly in an obvious way.

I'd changed too. But it was harder for me to see that difference in myself. I'd spent those four years, seven months, and eight days trying to keep everything the same. I realized now that it was an impossible goal.

It was harder for me than I had expected to say goodbye to the Worthingtons, but I left happy knowing both of their sons had survived the war.

It'd been ten times harder for Georgie to leave the Howes, though. He'd lived nearly as much life with them as he had with Mum and Dad. What a horrible realization!

And now, as much as I was looking forward to being reunited with my parents, I was fearing it. What if too much had changed for us to be a family again?

The train whistle sounded, announcing our arrival.

"I'm afraid I won't recognize them," Georgie whispered to me.

"You will," I said.

But before I stepped off the train with my brothers, I took a deep, reassuring breath. There were people everywhere. I swallowed, my gaze nervously jumping from person to person. People hugged. People laughed.

Then, I heard, "Hettie!"

I turned to the sound of the voice, the familiarity of it a prick in my brain. I saw Mum. It was like looking at myself: wavy brown hair, green eyes, the same exact height.

Mum was crying even before she reached us. Her hands cradled my face. Her hands jumped to Oliver's. Then to Georgie's. Mum circled back to me. Dad was there too, wearing the same brown hat he'd worn for years. He was giving Mum her moment, but he looked like he only had another few seconds in him before he'd burst.

He burst. His arms were around us all. After so long apart, we all stood on the platform and hugged.

"Let me get a better look at you three," Mum said through her tears.

Missing teeth. Taller. Older. Stronger.

She didn't mention smellier, but I knew she was thinking that too.

"I can't believe how different yet the same you three look," she said then. Mum's focus was on Georgie with these words.

Dad led us off the platform, toward home. There was an awkward silence for a moment until Dad said, "I, for one, can't wait to see the scar Oliver got sliding into home plate."

Oliver's face lit up. "You heard about that?" he asked.

But even as my brother asked, he was looking at me. I'd included it in one of my letters home. In my bag, I felt the weight of the stories I'd written down. The worn paper showed how well-read our memories had been while we were away.

"Oh, Hettie," Mum said, "Judy arrived home earlier today. She can't wait to see you."

I couldn't wait to see my best friend either.

"How about the zoo tomorrow?" Dad suggested.

I laughed at how our conversation was jumping around. I was sure it'd take time for our family to find its groove again. We had the time.

Georgie said, "I promise not to draw all over myself in coal this time."

My brother's comment stopped Mum in her tracks. Tears filled her eyes again before she laughed. "Good. Now, who's hungry for a Sunday roast?" she asked cheerfully, despite the fact it was a Saturday.

But who cared what day it was? All that mattered to me was that the gas masks were gone, bombs were no longer hitting London, the war was over, and my family was finally all together again.

A NOTE FROM THE AUTHOR

Hettie is a fictional character set in a very real and scary time in history during World War II. The London Blitz began on September 7, 1940. The city was bombed for 57 days and nights in a row. In all, the Blitz lasted eight months—until May 11, 1941. Throughout the nightly bombings, Germany dropped many bombs on the city. There were over five hundred tons (an elephant is seven tons, for comparison) of high-explosive bombs and thirty thousand fire bombs (also called incendiary bombs) dropped on London. The bombs destroyed two million homes and resulted in nearly sixty percent of London needing to be rebuilt.

I repurposed many real stories to create Hettie's story. Stories of graveyards being bombed, of a bomb shelter nearly being hit and the family inside needing to be rescued, and of people living underground in the tube stations. All are stories from real children who survived the Blitz.

The stories of getting fitted for masks, of classmates leaving school after devastating bombings, and of barrage balloons are real as well. Other details, such as the London Zoo's poisonous animals being terminated, the headlines from the posters and flyers, and the prime minister's radio announcement, are also factual. Of course, I took some liberties to fill in gaps and further bring the story to life. Any inaccuracies are my own for the purpose of storytelling.

When deciding the story I wanted to tell about the London Blitz, I considered various directions. But as soon as I read the stories of families being separated, with children leaving London and parents remaining behind, I knew this was the story I wanted to tell.

It broke my heart to learn of young children who were separated from their families and who didn't remember their parents when they finally returned years later. But I was happy to give Hettie and her family a happy ending. I do believe words are powerful, and I loved giving Hettie the opportunity to use them to keep her family together. I hope you enjoyed her story too.

GLOSSARY

air raid (AIR rayd)—an invasion by aircraft, especially for the purposes of bombing

Allies (AL-ize)—a group of twenty-six countries, including Great Britain, France, the Soviet Union, and the United States, that fought against Germany, Italy, and Japan during World War II

annex (AN-eks)—to add a smaller territory or country to a larger territory or country

blitz (BLITS)—an all-out attack

evacuation (ih-va-kyoo-AY-shuhn)—the removal of large numbers of people leaving an area during a time of danger; a *mandatory* evacuation means people are required to leave, while a *voluntary* evacuation means people can choose to leave

evacuee (ih-va-kyoo-EE)—a person who is removed from a place of danger

knackered (NACK-urd)—tired, exhausted

Luftwaffe (LOOFT-vahf-uh)—Germany's air force; the Luftwaffe was active from 1935 through 1946 and then brought back in 1956

ration (RA-shuhn)—to limit to keep from running out

MAKING CONNECTIONS

1. We see within the story that history often repeats itself. London was targeted with bombs during both World War I and World War II. When comparing the start of World War I to World War II, what two additional similarities are expressed to Hettie by her dad (in Chapter Two) and by Britain's prime minister (in Chapter Three)?

2. In Chapter Two, what memory do you think helps push Hettie to keep her family together at all costs? Why do you think it motivated her?

3. After Hettie and her brothers are evacuated to Clevedon, Hettie takes steps to help her brothers remember home. Provide three examples from the text to show the actions Hettie took. If you were in a similar situation, what would you do to remember home?

ABOUT THE AUTHOR

Jenni L. Walsh spent a decade enticing readers as an award-winning advertising copywriter before becoming an author. Her passion lies in transporting readers to another world, be it in historical or contemporary settings. She is a proud graduate of Villanova University and lives in the Philadelphia suburbs with her husband, daughter, son, cat, and dog. Jenni enjoys telling stories inspired by real life and has also written childrens books about Bethany Hamilton, Malala Yousafzai, the White Rose resistance during World War II, and the Revolutionary War hero Sybil Ludington. Learn more about Jenni and her books at jennilwalsh.com.